A SWIM

The Rhode Islander Who Refused To Drown

John K. Fulweiler, Jr.

Flood Tide Press llc
The Franklin Bakery Building
40 Mary Street, First Floor - Aft
Newport, Rhode Island 02840

Copyright © 2013 John K. Fulweiler, Jr.

All rights reserved including, the right to reproduce this book or portions thereof, in any form whatsoever. For information regarding same, contact Flood Tide Press llc.

Flood Tide Press llc, First Edition March 2013

Want to have this author speak at your event?
Contact Flood Tide Press llc at 1-800-383-MAYDAY.

MADE IN THE U.S.A.

Library of Congress Control Number:
ISBN 978-0-615-77688-0

Dedications

To the crew of United States Coast Guard Motor Lifeboat 47274 for keeping up the hope,

To the late Kenneth Gale Hawkes and Michael J. McHale, two admiralty attorneys and friends of the author for whom hope ran out far too soon, and

To anyone who is making their way on hope alone.

Disclaimer

    This story recounts the events of July 17-18, 2012 as understood by the author, John K. Fulweiler, Jr. As with any good story, allegiance to accuracy was important, but it was not permitted to be a hindrance. Some elements of this narration reflect the author's interpretation of circumstances based on his understanding and his vision of how things might have been had he been there to witness them. While an effort was made to be accurate, to capture quotations correctly and to otherwise convey the truest sense of the incident, this work is nonetheless a work of art reflecting the author's own characterizations and impressions. If you are in pursuit of the minutia of the incident, the author encourages you to research the copious press coverage and to pursue information from the United States Coast Guard via a Freedom of Information Act request. Any mistakes of fact or science are regretted, but this is a story, not a textbook.

--- John K. Fulweiler, Jr.

There is a great quote apparently attributed to the American psychologist, Abraham Maslow, about how he would swim toward land even if it was a thousand miles away and he'd hate the person who'd give up. There's a lot to like in that kind of thinking.

Chapter One

Joe Gross is a funny sort. He's that kind of guy you can't quite place. You want to maybe label him as a blue collar fellow who's done alright, but there's something else there. A spark of neuron and sound of whirling gears is present in his quick responses. He's got a good memory, rattling off the names of friends, colleagues and distant pals without a blink or fumbling pause. He'll squint at you hard over a dumb question answering bluntly without inflection and lean back and paw at his scalp when you ask a good one. His directness is refreshing and seems to fit him. Things are "yes" or "no" with Joe and when he elaborates it's not to hear himself talk. If he'd liked school, my bet is he'd be a surgeon or a law partner. There's an easy air of knowingness about him that probably never got to bloom like it would've if he'd gotten the academic traction.

Physically, he has the build of a NASCAR fan without the bulk. A solid softness at around six feet. Capable, not threatening, but not a mark either. His short white hair is in the familiar holding pattern of a fifty something year old. He sees the barber every ten days. They make the same jokes about the same things and they both know they're doing it, but it still makes them laugh. There's a ruddiness creeping outward from his nose. It's the windburn rash of the serious offshore fishing crowd brewed from a tonic of salt air and sun. Sometimes he'll break character raising both hands to demonstrate something with a sound effect like "whoomp" and "bam". He did just that when he told me how the Coast Guard picked him out of the ocean after he'd been swimming for eleven hours.

"When their boat got next to me, I said, 'guys I got nothing'," Gross says intensely. "And they just poofffgrabbed me," he raises his arms in lifting motion. "And then booom, right in the boat," he explains opening his hands like he was dropping something. "And that was it, it was over."

Eleven hours of swimming. Naked. No lifejacket. No flotation device. In ocean waters twenty-eight degrees cooler than his body temperature. Alone and with less than ten percent of his body mass poking out of the water, the chances of being found were horrifyingly dismal. But Joe was found and that's what's truly remarkable. Yes, Lady Luck took him by the arm, but on the other arm was a series of life experiences and determination that made all the difference. And as Joe won't let you forget he needed to get himself through eleven hours before Lady Luck stepped onto the dance floor.

This book is about Joe Gross and how he beat the ocean's best efforts at killing him. To me, it's as remarkable as any legendary mountain ascent, as inspiring as any biblical quest and as stirring a tale of survival that you'll find. In addition to unfolding Joe's experience in his own words, this book is about some of the things that Joe did that he believes resulted in him living and not dying. It's about sharing the mental reasoning Joe Gross relied on to keep himself alive. It's about how Joe was able to shed the emotional side of the moment and carry himself forward through sheer grit of spirit and willful determination. It's a testament to what we are capable of if we are willing to fight.

I am in utter awe of Joe's accomplishment and have spent many a moment asking myself whether I would've survived. I'm not sure. I'm just not sure. I do know now, that with the memory of how Joe approached this moment, I'm better prepared and more confident of my survival whether that be in the ocean's open waters, or, the troubled waters that litter a lifetime.

Chapter Two

July 17, 2012 was a Tuesday. One of those long, languid weekdays where the office worker winces in dismay at the golf game he's missing, the vacationer scoots low in the sun chair, and beach traffic clogs Rhode Island's southern highways. One newspaper reported the summer weather as being "built on clean, baking heat." Across the coastal waters, it was that sort of booming New England high where the sun and sea smack together in a blinding glare of dappled light and salt spray. Temperatures at Logan Airport peaked at 97 degrees, a red hair short of a record.

As if taking a pitch from the day's tune, the news was slow. The choice of vice-presidential candidates led the national headlines with plunging lobster prices capping the regional broadcasts. A small story, low in the Boston Globe reported that an association assisting families with missing children had reached a conclusion in an April disappearance of a toddler from a local beach. The girl, they reasoned, was swept out to sea and drowned. I don't think Joe saw that article, and I don't think it would've changed anything about the Tuesday fishing trip he'd planned. That people drown in the ocean, in pools, in lakes and in rivers is background noise to summertime fun in the United States. Still, the statistics are pretty gruesome.

Pick a weekend, any weekend. How about a random weekend in mid-June, 2012? In that otherwise nondescript two days, twenty-five people drowned in this Country's waters. The deceased were a mixed lot. There was a swimmer in the surf off a Pensacola Beach, a boy on the coastline near Atlantic City, a middle aged guy who fell overboard and a fifty-six year old who swam into the warm Gulf waters and couldn't keep himself afloat. People died in pools, ponds, lakes and rivers and at country clubs, resorts, and state parks. And that's the gritty numbers from just one random summer weekend scroll outward and the statistics get even scarier.

For instance, in a recent four year period, there were over 3,500 drowning deaths annually in the United States --- that's about ten deaths a day. Among America's youth, drowning almost culls as many of them as car accidents. Worldwide, drowning wins a Bronze medal as the third leading cause of unintentional deaths with an estimated 380,000 drowning deaths each year. To put that 380,000 deaths in perspective, that's nearly six times the number of total dead and wounded in the American Revolution, almost double the number of combat fatalities in the Civil War, three times the number of U.S. military deaths in World War I and about one hundred thousand more deaths than those U.S. citizens killed in combat in World War II.

Boating isn't any better and the statistics are equally grim. In 2009, seventy-five percent of all fatal boat accidents were as a result of a drowning. And worse, if the victim wasn't wearing a life jacket (like Joe), there was an eighty-four percent chance of drowning. In 2011, Rhode Island had twenty-six reported boating accidents with two deaths, Massachusetts had forty-six accidents and nine deaths, Connecticut had forty-two accidents and eight deaths, and Maine had forty-eight accidents and eleven deaths. It starts to make you think that the experts might be right about commercial air travel being safer, huh?

But for Joe, boating is as natural as anything. To him, the easy movements of starting his boat's engine, slipping the lines and motoring out of the harbor and into the wide expanse of the Atlantic Ocean is nothing. It's what he does. And why shouldn't that be the case? Chronologically speaking, man's involvement with the ocean is neatly linear. African cave drawings depict humans swimming, ancient anaglyphs from the depict soldiers escaping enemies by crossing rivers and the Greeks maintained a vigorous maritime trade for thousands of years. Joe is simply following in the aquatic pursuits that have always interested mankind. Alone or with friends, Joe doesn't seek ocean time to impress a girlfriend or fill a social media site. He keeps all those images to himself. "I just like being out there," he'll tell you. "I like doing stuff on my own and landing dinner." Indeed, it's an old fashioned sentiment, but in our world of voyeurs competing for electronic replies and mentions and Tweets, there's a forgotten pleasure to involving yourself in the scenery. Joe accumulates accomplishments like the rest of us post pictures online of packaged vacations and scheduled family affairs. For Joe, a day's fishing in the Atlantic Ocean eclipses the many risks. The flash of fin and curl of ocean wave are as much a lure as anything he'll cast into the sea.

The thing with drowning, though, is that it's a wicked way to go. It's a great big short circuit that forces the human body into counterintuitive responses.

If you live or work around the ocean, you may possess a sense as to what it'd look like if someone drowned, but you're probably wrong. You're likely tainted by Hollywood's images of the flailing and sputtering drowning victim and you rely on your own experiences. Every deadly encounter we face in life, you reason, is accompanied with a reaction. Whether it's a shout for help or the holler of someone in distress, you gather with friends around the poolside grill comforted by conditioning that you'll hear the kids if something goes wrong. We subconsciously believe that like a burn or a fall, we'll hear or see the panic of someone drowning.

Unfortunately, that's just not the case.

On the telephone, Francesco A. Pia, Ph.D's voice is that confident mix of Westchester hardness and scholarly wisdom. When he talks, you feel like you should be scribbling notes because what he's saying is so startlingly contrary to your own conventional wisdom. It's like you want to capture his words so that you can quote him later when someone tells you "no way."

"Water crises," he explains "are best looked at by breaking them down into two aspects. You have the person in distress and you have the person who's drowning. The difference between the two is very small. It comes down to whether someone is positively or negatively buoyant and that's a function of tidal air, the amount of air left in someone's lungs after they breathe out."

Dr. Pia should know because he's made a career out of studying drowning. More accurately, he's devoted forty-five years of effort toward reducing swimming related facilities. His resume runs into multiples of pages with publications, professional committee appointments, training aids and lifeguard experience. In developing training programs for teaching how to recognize a drowning person, Dr. Pia filmed countless drowning incidents and their associated rescues. And still, what he says seems sadly novel as if the message he preaches is like an outgoing tide sweeping unnoticed past the beach goers and poolside revelers.

"A swimmer in distress is someone who is negatively to positively buoyant," Dr. Pia continues. "There's some swimming or floating ability and they're able to keep their mouth above the water's surface so they're able to shout or wave for help. The problem is that Hollywood has taken this distress category and turned it into an all-encompassing drowning scenario and that's just not accurate."

It was in 1959 when Dr. Pia first became a lifeguard at New York's Orchard Beach. Recognizing that his on-the-job training seemed highly ineffective sparked an interest in developing a signal detection theory for understanding when someone was drowning.

"You'd see people," he says, "just standing around and not calling for help right next to someone who drowned. They just never knew because the human's physiological response to drowning is instinctive. It just takes over when the brain perceives you're not getting enough air to breathe. Your arms extend partially or fully out from your sides and you press down in an effort to leverage your mouth above the water. To the extent your mouth gets above the water, you gulp for air and then sink again. The instinctive drowning response forces your body into pushing the arms downward and sucking in air leaving no room for shouting or waving for help and the cycle only takes twenty to sixty seconds before you've drowned."

That the victim is trapped by instinctive forces is a horrifying aspect of drowning that likely contributes to a large percentage of fatalities. We're so conditioned to think that the body reacts to drowning in a certain way when, in fact, it doesn't. Despite John Lennon's seemingly sage statement about how when someone's drowning, they scream, there's almost never a shout for help because the body's ability to form words is overrun by the priority to breath. Studies show that drowning is a hauntingly silent event. Drowning victims rarely if ever wave for help because instinct forces their hands down on top of the water's surface as they attempt to push themselves upward. And moving toward a life ring or reaching out to grab hold of a boat hook is impossible because the drowning victim has lost voluntary control of their arms. (This latter fact helps explain the stupefying reality that a majority of drowning deaths occur within a short distance of safety.) The hapless becomes victim to their own reflexive actions and once the process starts, it's almost impossible to remedy without outside assistance. Like a trapdoor sprung open, the victim is powerless to avoid the inevitable.

"Unless you can get your feet on the bottom, you're screwed," Dr. Pia says soberly.

If you don't believe that drowning is a muted horror, consider the fact that a little more than half of the children that die from drowning will do so within yards of a parent. And worse still, in a large percentage of those instances, the adult will recount that they saw the child drown, but didn't realize what was happening.

It's worthless to attempt to describe the sense of drowning from an emotional standpoint. To try and do so is to try and capture a moment so fraught with sensation and horror that its mere telling rounds its edge and softens its impact. It's a little like the observer effect in quantum mechanics where the academic review of drowning changes what we perceive. No matter the labor applied to describing the mental processes surrounding drowning it always devolves into the cozy study of yet another way to die without the sensation of its gruesomeness.

To describe the drowning sequence as a traumatic experience is about as respectful and clinically accurate as you can get. So what happens physiologically? It starts with holding your breath. We've all done that and we all know that feeling of creeping panic when you need to breathe. From here we step off a ledge leaving most of us behind because what comes next are a series of mechanical motions that once started almost always result in death. The drowning sequence is as fatal as climbing over the bridge's rail and plunging downward.

Once the victim can no longer hold his breath, water pours into the victim's trachea inducing larynx spasms which close and open the windpipe entrance. This psychological response results in an anoxic condition and the loss of oxygen retards the brain's function and soon a cycle of aspirations begin in concert with the spasms. The victim suffers a sequence of anoxic panic interspersed with inhalations of seawater. Ultimately, the laryngospasms cease as the lungs fill with seawater resulting in complete anoxia. With seawater choking the lungs, the body's life-giving exchange of gas between the lung's membranes can no longer take place and your organs rapidly shut down from lack of oxygen. Concurrently, the salty brine in the lungs removes large amounts of water from the blood through osmotic pressure leading to heart failure.

Despite the gritty science of its method, literature seems to have a long romance with drowning. Shakespeare's Ophelia is a good starting point with Charles Dickens and a slew of Victorian authors also in the running. I sense history suffers from a belief that drowning was sort of an easy way to go be it in the literature or, paintings such as John Millais's The Death of Ophelia which arguably embraces the moment of drowning as something poetically valuable. The problem, of course, is that under the unblinking sky of reality, drowning is far from an easy death.

In a lawsuit involving a young child's death, a medical expert testified that drowning is anything but painless:

> The pathophysiology of drowning begins when the mouth and nose first become submerged in the water. At that point in time, the first reaction is to voluntarily breath hold [sic] to avoid aspirating water. The carbon dioxide tension then builds up to a point where you can no longer voluntarily avoid the sensation to breathe.
>
> At that point in time you start to take a breath and when you get water in the oral pharynx, that water stimulates the larynx to go into laryngospasm to further protect the airway from aspiration of water. And as a result you try to breathe but you can't because you are totally obstructed. It's as though someone were suffocating you or you put a clamp on your trachea.

As a result, you will build a tremendous negative pressure within your chest as your diaphragm tries to pull in air, which you can't, or water. And as a result the intercostal muscles will sink into the chest rather than rise. This causes a great deal of pain and discomfort of pain and suffering and this process lasts for a minute and a half to two minutes.[1]

Death from submersion typically occurs in less than two minutes. Football games are won and lost in two minutes. A lot of you could run a quarter mile or the length of about four football fields in two minutes. It's all relative, unless you're drowning and then it's undoubtedly a lifetime.

Drowning is a very personal journey with the victim locked into a spiraling event that can't be broken unless positive buoyancy is revived. "It's a terrifying and very painful experience," Dr. Pia says confidently. "The water is suffocating you. I can't think of a worse way to die except maybe by fire."

You want to think that as Joe rounded the coastline heading for Block Island on that sun-dappled day he didn't know any of this, but you'd be wrong. Joe had been a paramedic for many years and knew full well the horrors of drowning. He just didn't think about it much.

"Hell, man," he says grinning. "It was my day off and I was going fishing!"

---

[1] DRD Pool Service v. Freed, 416 MD 46 (MD App. 2010).

Chapter Three

It was a late winter night in the 1980's in the resort town of Saratoga Springs, New York. The season had begun to change just enough so that the warmer daytime temperatures made the snow heavy. If you'd looked hard enough you'd have seen the occasional green bud on the big maples that dot the region. The local maple syrup production was in full swing. It was nighttime and a fat moon hung over the town and flashed bright off the wet snow.

Joe was in Saratoga for the weekend. It was a weekend of snowmobiling with friends through canopies of trees and across untouched snow that blanketed the nearby valleys. Joe was on his own snowmobile, a fast, belt driven machine that whisks its rider along at speeds in excess of fifty-five miles per hour (the national highway speed limit back then). In the moonlit woods with friends streaking through dimly-lit trails and across swathes of lunar-lit frozen lake, Joe and his friends were in a distinctly different position than today where a web of communications makes it hard to separate yourself from friends, family and emergency assistance. In the early 1980's there were no cell phones, no instant messaging and no internet. An established doctor or successful executive might carry a pager whose primitive beeping indicated the office was looking for them. Alone in the upper reaches of New York State, Joe and his friends were more isolated, more cutoff from the civilization than you or I can imagine. Without really working at it, it'd be almost impossible today to place ourselves in as remote circumstances. (I'm told, however, that if you can cart yourself to Hinsdale County, Colorado, the U.S. Geological Service promises you'll be in the most remote location in the lower forty-eight states and it might just mimic the electronic void of a late winter night in upstate New York.)

Joe had finished high school a few years back. As he explains, high school partying eclipsed his academics and he'd stumbled into young adulthood blinking and looking around. Academics aside, Joe had been fortunate in that he'd found himself a passion. He loved the outdoors. In between disco and girls and summer hookups, an older neighbor had wetted Joe's appetite for the simple pleasures of stomping across an open field in the early morning. Joe learned how to fish the freshwater eddies of New England's backcountry. He learned how to hunker low in his blind and wait for a descending brace of ducks. He learned the tricks and methods that'd served to keep the earliest settlers alive during the harshest of seasons. The sensation of a bigmouth bass's rolling tug and the splash and sparkle of a rainbow trout proved far more addictive than the passing highs of teenage rebellion. In time, and something he can only appreciate in hindsight, what lessons Joe didn't learn in high school he'd augmented with practical knowledge. He'd become, in the vernacular of the region, a Swamp Yankee.

Each fall in Ashaway, Rhode Island, you can find the Swamp Yankees Festival celebrating the traditional arts of colonial living and keeping alive an expression that many have thought would have passed into history. In the 1963 journal of American Speech, the esteemed Ruth Schell described as Swamp Yankee with a definition worthy of one of Captain James Cook's Easter Island's biological observations.[2] She observes the classic Swamp Yankee as being stubborn, but well respected in the community and fortifying a lack of formal education with his own pursuits and experiences.

What Joe lacked in monetary advantage, he made up with an eagerness to learn. He was proud of his New England

---

[2] Ruth Schell, "Swamp Yankee," *American Speech*, 1963, Volume 38, No.2 (The American Dialect Society, Duke University Press), pp. 121-123.

birthplace, proud of his hands-on talents and like the many before him confident in his abilities. You had to be. With 9,900 miles of coastline, biting winters and rocky soil, New Englanders develop a depth of fortitude not easily matched.

Joe and his friends could reach their fastest speeds along the lake's surface where the frozen waters stretched for hundreds of acres. In the early 1980's lots of people enjoyed snowmobiling across these passages and it'd become a popular pastime. It wasn't without risk. Weighing over five hundred pounds without a driver, a snowmobile requires at least six to eight inches of blue ice to keep it from breaking through. The problem was that traveling at fifty-five miles per hour you're covering something like eighty feet a second making it difficult to adjust to changing ice conditions. In a lot of instances, by the time a snowmobiler knows they're on bad ice, it's too late. If Joe had asked around, he probably would've learned about how twenty-six year old Elizabeth Barrow had broken through the ice in 1980. She'd broken through right near where Joe was snowmobiling, her machine slowly spiraling into the darkened depths, tail first and with its headlight still lit. Remarkably, Elizabeth had clawed and splashed long enough to pass her two year old daughter to her snowmobiling companions before she succumbed.[3] In very cold water, a human has one to two minutes of lucidity before becoming physically unable to remain afloat.

Joe was making good money. Too good, maybe. In high school his first desire was to go to Vietnam, but the war had moved on by the time he was of age. "Vietnam," he tells you in

---

[3] The horror of that scene tightens this author's chest and I hope in some very small measure that this text helps highlight Ms. Barrow's brave actions as a testament to the awesome power of a mother's love and of the sheer will of the human spirit. I suggest to you that Ms. Barrow proved that indeed: *"Amor est vitae essential."*

a rarely serious tone of voice, "would've really been where I could've tested myself. Once you get through the fear, you become a machine, you know? I've read a lot about this, about how war is the crucible. You figure out pretty quick who you are and what you can do when someone's trying to kill you." So with Vietnam having passed him by, he went to work at Electric Boat. "Everyone did, man. That's the way it was. I wasn't a college kid then and I didn't have the means to go to college. It was as simple as that. So I chose to follow in my father's footsteps. I regret it, really do. I should've gone into the military. It's a very honorable thing, you know. It would've meant something to me, instead of just making a paycheck."

But it was the Ronald-Regan era, and Joe was a kid making pockets full of cash and partying hard. "You don't understand," he says. "I was skiing and snowmobiling every weekend. I bought a new Mazda RX7 right off the dealer's lot in cash. There were nightclubs and girls. You know, typical blue collar kid with some money stuff. To be honest, those years were all sort of a blur."

The Saratoga winter night had burned off the beer buzz pretty quick and Joe recalls that their small group had turned toward the lake's edge to make their way home. He was trailing the pack and was the last to zip from the lake's middle, toward the shoreline's edge. As he neared the shoreline bank where the frozen reeds and rushes had been flattened by his friends before him, his machine lurched, pitched upward and dropped away. In an instant, he was flailing in the dark water. His one-piece snow suit, snow boots and gloves sucked up the ice water like one of those miracle towels on late-night television. A gallon of freshwater weighs around eight pounds and within seconds the weight of his clothing made movement almost impossible. Pounding his hands on the top of the water's surface, he could feel his feet touching and slipping on the lake floor beneath him. Joe twisted and grabbed at the dry plant stalks clustered near the lake's edge, but they cracked and split in the dry night air. He fell backwards into the water and he heard the tinkle of ice scattering across the top of the circle of ice that corralled him.

He was so physically close to the lake bank where the water depth went from thirty plus to a couple of feet that the situation seemed almost ridiculous. Ridiculous until he realized he was going to die. That memory of death walking up and sitting on its haunches right next to him is vivid. "It was there, man" he says with a matter of fact conviction. "I just knew that that was it, this was how I was going to die. I mean, it's the middle of the night and I just fell through the ice. I couldn't move. I couldn't do anything except sort of settle backwards." He remembers turning and watching the bright beam of his snowmobile' headlight arcing below him as the machine twisted downward through the lake's depths. He remembers it sinking fast and how the red taillight got smaller and smaller and then disappeared. "It was like one of those old black and white television sets where after you shut it down there's this little dot that gets smaller and smaller and then disappears. I didn't know what to do, but die and I kept thinking whether it would hurt or not," he says.

His feet were facing the lake's edge and he was lying backwards slowly settling downward like he was making a snow angel on the water' surface. He remembers seeing his friend ahead of him waving and hollering at him. "He just started yelling at me. Really loud. Trying to snap me out of it, I guess. He was cursing and everything and telling me to get moving. It was the only thing he could do, just yell at me to try and move toward him so that he could pull me onto the bank and it was like, I don't know, I just started moving. It's easy to die when you think about it and all of a sudden seeing him there, I just started moving and I got close enough where they could wade in a little and grab me and that was it. I didn't die."

There's an abruptness to the way Joe talks about death. There's no fuzzy hesitancy. It's a logical outcome to a circumstance the same as posting a letter or hammering a nail. There's no doubt that the person Joe was on that cold evening in the late 1980's was not the same person that spent eleven hours in Block Island Sound in the summer of 2012. We change over time, but we also learn and what we learn sticks with us. Sure, the array of Joe's neurons that remembered that cold winter night two decades past were dusty with age, but they bounced back and started waving and shouting when Joe popped up, blinked his eyes clear of seawater and watched his boat skimming away from him on a summer's day in 2012.

"I mean I never really dwelled, you know, on that night" he explains. "It was like it was something that happened and I guess I just realized then that you can go right up to death and, you know, not die. That was something I learned that probably helped me here. I learned you have to fight. No one's coming in the water to help you. You gotta get out of there yourself."

Chapter Four

Rowing associations, colleges, and sailing teams often require you pass a swimming test. Basically you swim a few lengths of pool and tread water for ten minutes. Go spelunking around the internet and you'll see various websites claiming Navy S.E.A.L.S. tread water for seven hours. Joe Gross treaded water for eleven hours without any assurance of survival and he was fifty-one years old.

Joe's feat can only be understood by knowing something about falling overboard. Not falling overboard from your skiff on a summer day and scrambling back, but falling overboard and watching your boat motor away. That is, a circumstance where you fall overboard and you are not promptly recovered. Remarkably, falling overboard is the single most frequent cause of boating deaths whether it's a weekend boater or an Alaskan crabber. It's not the act of falling overboard that kills you it's either the lack of a lifejacket or cool water temperatures or a combination of the two that prove fatal.

The frightening scenario of falling overboard is not uncommon. No amount of romanticism will ever change the fact that your boat is an inanimate object. It will not turn around nor clutch out of gear. A vessel underway and making way will continue to do so until it runs out of fuel, wind or water. People are lost overboard from commercial fleets, cruise ships and recreational vessels. Many are safely recovered with little more than the scar of soggy socks and a good story by which to remember the event. Others are less fortunate. Between 2000 and 2010, approximately 170 commercial fishermen died as a result of falling overboard which is about thirty-one percent of all commercial fishing deaths during that period. What's startling about that last statistic is that a not one of those fishermen was wearing a lifejacket underscoring the seeming death sentence when you fall into the open ocean without some form of flotation assistance. Statistics from other boating sectors support this reality. In 2011, the American Waterways Operators reported that a crewmember is four times more likely to die if they go overboard without wearing a personal flotation device. During that same year in New England alone, twenty nine people fell overboard from recreational vessels without a lifejacket and every one of them died. The 2011 recreational boating season in Maryland resulted in twenty overboard fatalities with eighteen of the deceased found without a lifejacket. Similarly, the boating mecca of Florida reported in 2010 that falling overboard represented the largest proportion of recreational boating fatalities.

When people fall overboard from a cruise ship, they're almost always not wearing a lifejacket and they seem to almost always die. There are scant statistics regarding the number of cruise line passengers that fall overboard. No doubt the billion dollar plus industry is not keen on seeing such numbers aggregated.

It's easy to talk about falling overboard from the clinical standpoint of statistics, but much harder and downright frightening to consider the emotional impact. Few circumstances give rise to a greater sense of disconnect than being separated from your vessel. There is an overwhelming starkness in the vision of a single person bobbing amidst the ocean's lunging movements. From the victim's perspective, there is an unbound hellishness in having your senses limited to a dome of sky and water's surface. When Pip, the young boy in Herman Melville's Moby Dick is conscripted to the whaleboat, he jumps overboard after sighting a whale.[4] In that scene, Melville beautifully captures the moment by describing Pip as being left stranded in the "awful lonesomeness" of the ocean. An "awful lonesomeness," indeed.

---

[4] Herman Melville (1851). Moby Dick. New York: Harper & Brothers.

In a 2006 article reporting on a Dutch sailor who fell overboard in the Atlantic, the New York Times accurately explains that the "worst nightmare" of any sailor is "watching helplessly as their boat sails away from them." Like the inevitable conclusion of a folded wing to a pilot, falling overboard is the ever present haunt for the solo sailor. With no one to drop the sails, or, idle the throttle, the solo sailor can never reclaim his craft and is cruelly abandoned to the elements. Although the conditions were benign with calm seas and a decent water temperature, a thirty-six year old man who fell from a vessel in Australian waters in July, 2012 was never found. In the words of an Australian Maritime Authority spokesperson: "The conditions are good for searching but, I stress, for anybody in the water it would be a challenging survival situation."

When Joe Gross surfaced and saw his boat motoring away from him, he says: "I knew I was a dead man. That's the first thing, I thought. This was the ocean and no one gets out of this kind of situation."

But sometimes, they do.

For instance, in 2011, the transatlantic winning sailor, Florence Arthuad, fell overboard from her sailboat while attempting to relieve herself in the Mediterranean. Her unabashed statement to the media was simple and precise: "I quite simply fell into the water while preparing to take a pee." Thankfully for Ms. Arthaud, she retained her cellphone and was able to call her mother. Although reported to have suffered hypothermia, she was recovered approximately two hours later. For Joe, however, when he splashed free of the foaming wake of his vessel, there was no cell phone to keep clear of the water. He was starkly and singularly alone.

And there are others with seeming remarkable tales of falling overboard and having survived. Almost twenty years ago, a British Columbia manfell overboard from a ferry. The late evening ferry was crossing a local Bay and the ferry crew was apparently oblivious to their lost passenger. Reports of the event describe the man as having spent the next eight hours treading water without a lifejacket and drifting between the islands until he was rescued. More recently, a New York private pilot ditched his plane into one of the Great Lakes and alleges he spent some twenty hours treading water without a lifejacket. Both events have the sort of miraculous qualities attributable to Joe's endeavor until you realize the distinguishing (and lifesaving) difference between these events and Joe's. From the reports, it appears both the British Columbian man and the pilot may have been overweight. While Madison Avenue might wrinkle its waxed lip, extra weight is a lifesaving quality.

"We call them 'floaters'," Dr. Pia, the doyenne of the drowning process, explains. "Some people simply have a natural buoyancy, partial or otherwise, which allows them to stay afloat while deploying a great deal less energy than what it might take you or me. It's all about lung capacity and body mass." Another expert puts the advantage of being heavy more bluntly describing "fatness" as providing significant buoyancy making it easier to float and keeping the body insulated.

"But that wasn't me," Joe says incredulously as I lay my notes on the table. "Look man, I was just wrapping up my divorce and I was doing all this biking and I was in the best shape of my life. It was Mountain Biking and I was really into it and so, yea, being in shape helped, but I wasn't overweight or anything. I look different now some because I've been drinking a lot of beer lately, but trust me I was in the best shape I'd been in since like fifteen years ago. I worked at keeping afloat, struggled at it. I'm not a, what'dya call it? A floater? No way, guy, wasn't me. Wish it had been."

I think he's right. Moreover, unlike the conditions in the two prior incidents, Joe struggled against rough seas making it unlikely he was able to rely on any sort of natural buoyancy.

In the annals of seamanship instruction, there are procedures and processes to employ when someone falls overboard. There are symposiums, safety meetings and committee reports dedicated to honing crewmember recovery techniques. With respect to vessel handling in such situations, there is the Q-Turn, the Anderson Turn, the Williamson Turn and the Scharnow Turn all designed to quickly reroute the vessel to the location of the overboard alarm. There's even an international signal flag "Oscar" with its bright red and yellow stipe used to signal to others that a vessel has lost a person overboard. Many vessels are equipped with man overboard poles that can be deployed instantly to mark the person's location. The Annapolis Book of Seamanship provides six steps to follow in such circumstances beginning with avoiding panic and followed by keeping the overboard crewmember in sight.[5] This sailor's bible explains that losing sight of the crewmember can be disastrous because a human's head in the water possesses all the characteristics of a half-sunken coconut making it a very difficult target to identify. There's also the problem of spreading distance when someone falls overboard because even a vessel creeping along at a mere one knot an hour covers a hundred feet a minute!

The Annapolis Book of Seamanship's remaining four steps instruct the vessel to get buoyancy to the crewmember, make physical contact, stop the vessel and get the crewmember back aboard. In the airy space of a seaside yachting venue with attendees nursing free beers and munching snacks, these six steps convey a mechanical cleanliness which scrubs free the

---

[5] John Rousmaniere (1999).The Annapolis Book of Seamanship.New York: Simon & Schuster.

reality of such moments. The time it takes to awaken crew, the sails that must be dropped, the errantly thrown life ring, the haphazard line tossed with good intentions, but which wraps the wheel and all the other accompanying whips and whirls are neatly blotted from view by these six steps. However, the litany of sailors and crew who fall overboard from manned vessels and who subsequently drown stand as stark testament to the bleak reality that even with everyone working to get you back aboard and even with application of all the techniques and methods, it's a difficult proposition. And, of course, all of these teachings and sage advice assume that the fall overboard occurred from a vessel that is manned. That is to say, there's pitifully little instruction offered to the overboard victim. What's there to say?

While there's certainly no solace in the fact that when Herman Melville's Pip fell overboard, Melville wrote about the sea having drowned the poor boy's soul, there may be a teaching moment in that passage. Melville clearly possessed a sailor's sense of the frightening thoughts that must overwhelm the overboard crewmember. The immediacy of one's options being so suddenly whittled down to swimming or dying must surely have driven many to lose their wits and succumb to the odds. Melville's Pip is so scared he literally loses his mind which was something Joe reflects was very nearly an outcome that threatened to kill him even before his vessel motored over the horizon.

"I panicked at first, sure I did," he says. "I wasn't in the Bay or the harbor I was in the middle of freaking Block Island Sound. Shit, it was the Atlantic Ocean. There was nothing between me and Spain. It was like, well you're done for now and you start thinking of the dumbest shit you're going to miss. Like the cat. I mean, there I was thinking about my cat "Polar Bear" and I could feel this like rising fear all over me. Like how it wasn't going to see anyone again."

Physiologically, that surge of panic triggers the sympathetic nervous system which revs up in preparation for action. If Joe had been wired up, the amygdala region of his brain which controls fear would have been blinking bright with activity. Reduced to the pixilated images of a flat screen, Joe's brain would have been firing as colorfully as the Fourth of July fireworks he'd watched the week before. But somehow, Joe was able to control that rising tide. He was able to turn a flood tide of emotion and fear into a slack tide. I wondered how he had done it.

"Look, my EMT career I did for fifteen years," he explains with eye's widening. "I saw a lot of people panic over the dumbest stuff and over and over I saw that when you let all that adrenaline drive you into a dark place, it never helps. There's a primitive side to the human body and it's sort of programmed to just shut down if you let panic do its thing, you know? You go into shock, whatever. The thing is you stop thinking and thinking is the only thing I had. I didn't have a lifejacket or a cooler to hang onto, all I had was my brain. It was just like this basic learning I had that told me that if I panicked I was going to die, period. If I didn't panic and I got a plan and I stuck to my plan, maybe I wouldn't die. Yea, the odds were shit but what was I supposed to do just let myself drown?"

In the vernacular of the seasoned airline pilot I once shared a bar top with and who explained how he'd handle an aircraft emergency, Joe was going to keep trying to fly his plane right into the ground. Joe was never going to be accused of having given up. He wasn't going to let the only life preserving device he possessed, his brain, become clouded and unworkable with fear. Early on he made a decisive and, no doubt, extremely difficult decision to keep fighting and he did that by focusing on a plan. Developing a plan was Joe's lifeline. It was the floating cooler he could cling to and think about and rely on in trying to quite literally will himself out of the grim situation of being alone with night falling in the middle of hundreds of square nautical miles of ocean. It was Joe's plan that helped eclipse the grim reality of how hard it was going to be for rescuers to spot his half a coconut-sized head.

It would be a long night.

Chapter Five

In the lyrics of the song "Downeaster 'Alexa," Billy Joel sings that he's cruising through Block Island Sound. It's a song of loss and as much a tale of any of the Northeast's fishing fleets as it is the loss of Long Island's fishing industry. What were waters teeming with fish beyond our modern imagination, are now mere shadows of a glorious pelagic past. The once abundant fishery stocks are exhausted by overfishing, crowded out by the pollution of populated shorelines and mismanaged by bureaucratic oversight. It's a tale worthy of Joel's soulful voice.

Geographically speaking, Block Island Sound is that part of the Atlantic Ocean separating the shoreward coastline of the United States from an island colloquially referred to as the "Bermuda of the North." Perhaps the latter is an oversell, but Block Island is indeed a unique spot on the chart full of sweeping panoramas, good eats, a long history and a generous depth of water. A scant five miles long, it's an ancient "I-Was-Here" sign left in the Atlantic Ocean by the tilling movements of past glaciers. Verrazano reported its location in 1514, Captain Kidd strolled its shores, it was a neutral territory trading with both sides (incredibly) during the American Revolution, Amelia Earhart dove in its harbor and two Second World War aircraft carriers bore its name. Like a castle of sorts, the island's elevations run upwards of two hundred feet while the coastline is skirted by a boulder necklace making close-in navigation a tricky deal. In the summer, this patch of ocean rock is overrun with tourists. Red-faced parents trailing behind their suburban brood trudge the island's roadways staring in wonder at the vistas of open ocean. Mopeds buzz madly between the hubbub of Old Harbor and the recreational boating scene moored (and haphazardly anchored) in New Harbor. The locals wince and groan quietly eager for the first cool August evenings to arrive and displace the motley summer crowds.

The island has a unique shape. Raindrop or teardrop, take your choice. I like to think it's a teardrop falling from the edge of some long vanished glacier. Or a teardrop for all the vessels wracked against its shoreline, maybe. Perhaps instead, it's a teardrop for all the pain and suffering beset on its waters.

If you clear off your breakfast table and unfurl NOAA Chart number 13215 what you see is a long strip of coastline, Block Island and a whole lot of that lovely blue the government slathers around to represent the ocean. The United States Coast Pilot 2, Chapter 7 advises that Block Island Sound will "accommodate vessels of the greatest depth." It should know. The Coast Pilot is the absolute best use of your taxpaying dollars. It is a narrative of all coastline from Maine around and up the west side of Florida and it's neatly updated and maintained and chock full of commentary about anchoring locations, currents and all the things a boater needs to know.

The struggle for survival is not something unfamiliar to Block Island Sound. It's hosted scenes of gruesome loss with the 1907 collision between the steamer "Larchmont" and the schooner "Harry Knowlton" surely ranking as one of this Country's worst seafaring tragedies. The accounts of the February collision written in the stilted newsy language of the era describe an event of unmitigated horror. On a February night in the midst of the Sound and while most of the steamer's passengers were asleep, a sailing schooner carrying coal to Block Island and a passenger steamer bound for New York collided promptly sinking the schooner and rending a large hole in the steamer causing it to sink by the stern within minutes of the collision.

Occurring long before the fast response vessels of today and long before the ability to instantly communicate one's distress, the passengers and crew of each vessel were left alone to battle the elements. Many were clothed in light sleeping garments and the bitter freezing conditions created a scenario of unparalleled starkness. Bodies floated ashore on Block Island in gruesome frozen postures with one newspaper reporting that in many cases the victims looked as if "they were in the very act of fighting the fate that was in store for them."One crewmember so overcome by the prospect of having to endure the conditions reportedly plunged a knife into his neck and fell to the floor of the lifeboat. The few survivors suffered debilitating cold weather exposure and the graphic reporting of the subsequent pain and amputations is awesome in its crudeness. One hundred and fifty souls perished, and no doubt the waters of Block Island Sound rung loud that February evening with the slap and struggle of human life.

New Englanders endure their region's climate for the reward of sun dappled July days like the Tuesday Joe set out to do some fishing. The booming overhead blue of a summer day was like an interstate's persistent road signage urging the weary exit, eat and enjoy. Joe had planned to go fishing a day or so before.

"It wasn't anything big," he says with the look of someone explaining the obvious. "I go out there a lot. I just saw the weather was going to be good and figured I'd head out and try my luck."

Where he was going was a one mile or so sand shoal jutting off the northern edge of Block Island. If the island is a teardrop, the shoal runs from the narrow tip that sits atop the bulbous bottom outward in a direction toward the mainline about twelve miles away. Everyone with a rod and boat has different coordinates for where they like to fish along its edge which drops off steeply into the deep ocean. A lighted bell buoy rusted and dented with the abuse of riding through the Atlantic's onslaught is moored at the shoal's very northern reaches. There are lots of reasons for why the location is so good for fishing. Numerous sand eels, silversides, bunker and squid inhabit the varying depths and local structures making it a good feeding ground. Plus, you have the mix of tidal currents and varying water temperatures. Good stuff for big fish and the prized Sea Bass, Stripers and infamous, but equally prized Blue Fish gorge on its abundance. The North Rip is an equally irresistible fishing hole for the saltwater fisherman. That is, saltwater fishermen who know what they're doing.

Fishing the North Rip of Block Island requires a good deal of experience with the locale. This isn't plugging away for Flounder in the upper reaches of some protected water and if you don't possess an understanding of the depths, tidal currents and fishing techniques necessary for the area, you'll only have a sunburn and a fuel bill to remember your voyage from the mainland, if you're lucky. The unlucky get sucked into the shoal waters and capsized. One imagines a tidy living could be made salvaging the lost anchors of vessels that couldn't or didn't have time to avoid a change in tides or shift in ocean breeze and had to "cut and run" to avoid being set against the shallows. You need the right kind of boat and the right mix of talent and experience to safely fish the North Rip.

You can troll wireline outfits, drift with plastic setups, hook them with top water plugs, or rig a jig and wait. Like a stringed instrument, the combination of techniques that the North Rip will tolerate is seemingly endless making it a siren's call for the avid saltwater fisherman.

Joe owns his boat. He's owned a bunch of them because that's the nature of living on the coast. He ordered the Eastern 22 Lobsterman new and finished it out the way he wanted. Adding cleats, installing the radio, measuring for the rod holders, Joe rigged his twenty-two feet to catch fish. It's a journeyman's boat, condensed space powered by an efficient outboard that pushes it along at a cruising speed in the low twenty knots. To the uninitiated, it's a smaller version of a bigger lobster boat. For the motorist, it's the Mercedes E Class embracing all the good design aspects of the big 140 series in a smaller package.

The thing about this boat is that it fits Joe's personality. Of course he'd have a boat that's handmade in New Hampshire at the kind of place you can call ahead and they'll let you walk the production floor and talk to the company owners. The builder has a good reputation for building rugged vessels with good finishes and with like anything in the maritime sector, you buy the vessel with the attributes you value. Joe wanted a dry, downeast style lobster boat that was good in a head sea. He wanted a boat he could use to fish in the open ocean, not something for the coastal shallows. He named it "Rock Bottom."

Like any good New Englander with respect for the sea and the countless souls of past that plied these waters, Joe pays an almost spiritual homage to certain things.

"Don't whistle on a boat, don't like red skies at night, and don't change a boat's name," he tells me with a serious line of eye. "That's how it was with my boat's name. When I came up with the name it worked because I was pretty much only going to lobster and bottom fish with her so 'Rock Bottom' fit, you know? But then things, changed and I was going to do some chartering. Take people out fishing what have you, but when I ran the numbers it was a break even deal at best and so the name seemed to fit that plan, too. I don't know. I never painted the name on the boat so I guess I never committed to it, but it was her name and I'm not about to change it. Superstitious, I guess."

Joe says she handles well, and with her small forward cabin and a proud bow that springs upward I imagine she rides the seas better and drier than the open decks of the center consoles that populate the inshore fishing grounds. The old salts might complain about her small scuppers which allow water to drain off the deck and overboard. Too small a scupper, they'll tell you, and you can get dangerous amounts of seawater on deck that'll play havoc with your vessel's stability. It's also a narrow boat which while making her good running into a head sea, likely means she's tippy and will roll more from side to side than a boat with a greater width. More width equals more stability is the general rule. Interestingly, I've also read some grumblings about the low freeboard meaning the height of the sides of the vessel from the water's surface. You're low to the water when you're aboard, but, as Joe tells it: "It's a hell'uva lot easier to land a fish by yourself is what it is."

It's also a hell'uva lot easier to get pitched over the side.

Chapter Six

Joe lives in Westerly, Rhode Island. Where Joe's house is on a street with the name "Summer" which is as good as living on Maple Street or Oak Lane. It's quintessential American pavement and that it intersects with a main thoroughfare by the name of "Granite" only underscores the smell of apple pie, steamed lobster and porches with white lacquered chairs. Westerly is Rhode Island's southernmost town straddling the very edge of the Connecticut border. It suffers from an affiliation with Connecticut whereas most of the rest of the state aligns itself with Massachusetts. In Westerly, allegiances to the Patriots, Celtics and Bruins can't be so easily assumed; there's a fair share of Giants, Nicks and Ranger fans here too.

Like Block Island, Westerly puffs up in the warm summer months doubling its paltry population of about 22,000 for a three or four month period. People clamber out of Manhattan's canyons and train northward or navigate the I-95 corridor for the chance to stretch out on a Westerly beach. The long white beaches are famous among an equally long stretch of generations. Weekapaug Beach, Westerly Town Beach, Misquamicut State Beach, East Beach and Watch Hill Beach have been the bastion of vacationing families for years on end.

Joe Gross grew up in Westerly; physically and mentally. He met and married his wife here. His child was born at the local hospital. He's left and then returned here. When Joe drives you around Westerly, the native in him comes out strong. There's a lot of slow braking and gesturing as he points out the kinds of reminisces we all sort of cherish whether we have them or not. There's the butcher he's gone to since he was ten. "Used to be called 'Brunos," he says. "Now it's Westerly Packing. The place is like 100 years old. I don't buy my steaks anywhere else." There's the Midway for grinders. "Only place to get them," he says. "Awesome. Every time I go out on the boat, I got'ta hit Midway first and get a grinder. Roast Beef, extra mayo." There's "Gervasini's" with its painted plate-glass window, two-tone stone front, row of barber chairs and brown, three-panel Naugahyde sofa right out of 1962. "Mark or Jimmy," Joe says turning to me as if sharing a trade secret. "Either one of them gives a good cut, a shave too. I've been going there for years. That place has a lot of memories for me. Prom, a lot of Saturday nights, weddings, bunch of funerals." It's a seventeen dollar haircut; just pricey enough not to drive away the local traffic while still soaking the summer trade.

The sun hadn't yet rotated to the top of the dial that Tuesday when Joe wheeled his truck into the parking lot of the Westerly Yacht Club. He pulled the cooler with his Midway grinder and some ice from the bed and braced a six-pack of Budweiser under his arm and walked across the parking lot and down an aluminum ramp. His boat was bow in, two-thirds of the way along the floating dock. It was that kind of electrically powered mid-morning where all the imperfections a boat owner worries on an overcast day are blasted away by the sun. Every hull looked good. Every bit of chrome or brass, no matter how dulled or pitted with age, seemed to pop bright. Even the slow moving water rubbing its way past the resting hulls had a diamond-dappled appearance.

Nary any warning to how the voyage would unfold.

Joe stowed his cooler in the small cabin tucking it on the floor between the two forward bunks. He lowered his outboard engine into the water with a whine of the hydraulics. Like the stillness that settles across the New England landscape after a winter snowfall, a Tuesday in the middle of the summer is its seasonal cousin. Aside from the babble and gurgle of the water and the hawking craw of a passing gull, summer's sounds of merriment were on hold. Most boats were tucked in their slips recovering from the past weekend and awaiting the next. Most owners were tucked behind desks or working jobs eager for the week to end and the next weekend to begin.

Joe leaves his lines on the dock. Barefoot, he hops onto the dock and walks forward to unbend his bow line before padding to the stern freeing the spring and loosening the stern line.[6] He steps back on the gunnel and down onto the solidness of his boat's deck, bumps the engine into reverse, swings the wheel counterclockwise and nudges the stern clear of the dock's edge. A frothy purl of water laps around the transom and the boat pulls out of the slip, and pivots to port.

The Westerly Yacht Club is located on the Rhode Island side of the Pawcatuck River. Joe motors south past Mastuxet and Babcock Coves. He passes the old Frank Hall Boat Yard, the Lotteryville Marina and the Avondale Boat Yard, the place where took he delivery of his boat. He punches the throttle forward and gets a little lift at the bow and his wake starts trailing behind in a big, foaming streak. The Watch Hill Boat Yard passes to port and he cuts inside the channel marker and rounds Napatree Point close in like all the natives who know what they're doing do. He can smell the ocean. It's a smell he'd have mentioned liking if I'd been aboard.

And then . . . bam. There she is. The Atlantic Ocean. This big body of water represents forty-one million square miles of lunging seawater and twenty percent of the earth's surface. It's a picnic blanket of blue stretching out and curving over a distant horizon. Keep heading westward, Joe, and you'll land on

---

[6] By way of orientation, most ropes on a boat are called "lines." The "bow line" secures the front of the boat to the dock while the "stern line" secures the back (or "aft" in nautical parlance) portion of the boat to the dock. A "spring line" is a line running diagonally from either the bow or the stern to the dock and serves to keep the boat from moving forward or backwards.

the coast of Spain. It's just over there, 3,285 nautical miles to the west.

An ocean breeze has come up and with it comes a scalloped ripple to the ocean's edge. The surging sea grabs at particles of sunlight spinning and reflecting it back in brilliant sheens making every aspect of the day sparkle. Back on the mainland, four Delta flights report passengers finding sewing needles in their turkey sandwiches, the Backstreet Boys are recording a new album, and President Obama is watching a basketball game in Brazil. Where else would you want to be?

For Joe, Block Island angles off to his left or to port as anyone with any boating knowledge will tell you. It's about twelve nautical miles to the North Rip and Joe gets his boat up on a plane and cruises at a steady eighteen knots. There are two types of vessel hulls. There's a full-displacement hull like a tug or a cruise ship and a planning hull. A full-displacement hull has no pretension of speeds. They are the steady lumbering Beatles of ocean transit. They are the fishing trawlers, the tugs and the cruise ships that gently part the liquid medium as they move forward. And then there's the planning hull which is designed so that as the hull speed increases, the draft (or the amount of the vessel that's in the water) is decreased. Joe's boat was a planning hull that skipped lightly across the ocean's surface.

You steer Joe's boat from the right (or starboard) side. The shiny chrome wheel is mounted to the bulkhead that forms the aft section of the forward cabin. There's a gray set of engine controls and a plastic handhold mounted on the overhang above the steering position. It looks like the handholds you might find inside a car on the ceiling above the door except this one doesn't fold up on springs. It's just a white, weathered looking handle. A plain piece of ten inch injection molded plastic relied upon to keep you steady and inside the boat.

"It gets sort of hot sometimes," Joe explains. "And so what I do is sort of lean out a little over the gunnel, you know. I lean out past the cabin and into the breeze. I hold on here," Joe says reaching one hand above his head and grabbing at the plastic handhold in demonstration. He hangs on and leans outside the edge of this boat.

"I've always done it that way. It's a good way to cool off," he says grinning.

He was sitting against his lifejacket. Don't we all? I mean it's right there, slung across the back of the helmsman's seat. If I need it, the reasoning goes, I'll just grab it. What could go wrong? I remember a summer day twenty plus years ago running an employer's over-powered rigid hull inflatable out and around Beaver Tail Light at the end of Jamestown. I had a lifejacket slung across the seat just like Joe when I hit a funny patch of staggering waves and punched the nose of the inflatable into a green sea. The inflatable pivoted up and to the right and then down hard and a lens of green water punched over the bow and suddenly I was outside the hull. The water's wetness felt so foreign and shocking and the inflatable was ahead of me now and I was behind it. Five yards away then ten and almost twenty. The reality of the moment was overwhelming. I flailed upright and smacked the sea in an effort to chase down my ride. But, I was lucky. The engine kill switch snagged on some part of me as I'd twisted and fallen and the outboard motor shutdown. I paddled down the inflatable's wake and clambered back aboard. My adventure was over in less than thirty seconds.

It took Joe an hour of motoring to make the North Rip. There were a few other day boats nuzzling the edges of the sands trying to divine where the big fish were idling. The wind was stronger, but the water was still relatively smooth with only the hint of the gently rounded seas that tend to build in the afternoon.

Joe puttered. He idled back and ran along the western edge of the North Rip his hull tottering back and forth in the seaway. Nothing caught his eye. No flash of silvered tail, no particularly intriguing pattern of current. It was a day off and he motored around to Old Harbor, tied up and ate his sandwich, and drank a beer. He watched the girls, admired the lines of the grand sport fishermen that dwarfed his small ride, grinned like a kid at the day, and let the sun warm his New England bones. Its days like these that make you appreciate these waters. When you know how savage things can turn, how cold and dark the winter months will be, you tend to really sit back and soak in the pretty ones.

The day was unremarkable. Joe didn't meet anybody although a recent separation from his wife had him in that kind of mood. He'd been wrapped up in a sort of carefree return to his youthful spirit as of late. Yea, he was still sending the occasional text message to his wife letting her know his plans, but my sense was that for the most part he felt like he wasn't answering to anybody. No doubt it was an old sensation he hadn't touched in a while and maybe he'd gotten a little drunk on the feeling. A little drunk on the sense that he'd started a new chapter in his life when he should've known that new chapters aren't started at fifty-one; it's the same chapter it's just going to end differently. I don't know. It's speculation on my part, but I believe that at some point the Block Island daytrip wasn't unfolding how Joe imagined. Sure, it was fun, but you can only keep grinning at the day so long.

I've seen Joe and his wife together. I've watched her kindly eyes and seen the smile as she recounts all the trips they'd made to Block Island together. Maybe it's a romantic notion, but I know that if it'd been me, there's only so much sun and solitude that I could embrace before I began to miss sharing the moment. It's hard to soak up the beauty of things on your own particularly where the seascape is littered with past memories. And so, I imagine that Joe cast off and spun his tidy yacht around and made his way back home with a sense of something. Maybe it wasn't regret, but it was something. A wistfulness, perhaps. Time lost. Choices made. Decisions that once their lever is pulled, become hard to undo.

So there it was. A man in the midst of a fairly significant life change trying to enjoy a day in what arguably, I'm sure, would've ranked high as the prettiest places on earth that silly Tuesday in the middle of the summer on the western edge of the Atlantic Ocean. The weather changed when Joe rounded the North Rip and pointed the bow toward home. An ocean breeze had come hurrying back from some distant point and the sea surface was sloppy and sometimes curling bright as the water curled and foamed on top of itself. Joe's vessel hipped and heaved along in the changing conditions making the deck shift and plunge. Typical weather, he'll tell you, still a beautiful day.

As near as Joe and I can figure, he was almost exactly mid-way between Block Island's North Rip and Napatree Point. If you unfurl NOAA Chart 13215, it's a fair guess that he was just past the "S" in the "Block Island Sound" designation. That is, he was almost half-way home. He was half way to his short stretch of dock and pick-up truck and his friends and his fractured family when he intersected with a bobble of seawater that changed his life. Who knows where that funny line of sea came from, or, what initiated it and don't begin to try and calculate the odds of Joe's vessel catching that wee wave at just the right angle and trajectory to drop the bow down hard, lift the stern around and decelerate sufficiently so that Joe was lifted and tumbled into the ion-charged summer air. There were no other boats around and all Joe remembers of the preceding moments is a sense of isolation and the sweeping vistas of the ocean. He doesn't remember seeing a change in the wave patterns. Waves come and go, lift and curl, shine bright, shine dull and some splash and some slip past hurrying away to some distant shoreline. There's a visceral memory of the sensation of his hand wrenching free from the little white steady handle above his head; the plastic rubbing fast and course across his palm. He remembers the tumble into the air, the cool break of seawater wrapping him tight and short circuiting his emotions, the surge of foamy sea and a salty taste in his mouth. He remembers splashing at the sea's surface and scissor-kicking himself around and trying to orient. And there's a whole squadron of his neurons burned with the image of the stern of his vessel waggling away, like a fleeing steed unfettered from its rider, and he remembers well that swell of hopelessness as hard hitting as a shotgun blast to the chest.

"It was devastating," he says gnawing on the edge of his lip. "It's like being in a car accident and just watching that tractor-trailer swinging toward you and knowing, shit, I'm going to die. Actually, it was worse, really. I mean, it was like I felt that moment was in slow motion so I had time to really realize what was happening. This wasn't going to be quick and neat, you know?"

But he had a plan.

Chapter Seven

What would you do? Honestly. I mean you're in the Atlantic Ocean no less than seven miles to the nearest shoreline with night falling. No life jacket. No phone. No overturned hull to clamber aboard and shiver until help arrives. No one even knows you're in the drink. That was the crazy thing. Somehow, in the year 2012 where cellular connections and data links are ubiquitous, Joe had managed to place himself in as remote a setting as he'd been some thirty years prior in a winter month in upstate New York.

Joe swears he didn't cry, confesses to babbling aloud at what a fool he'd been for not wearing a life jacket, swears he didn't pray 'cause he isn't all that religious and insists he knew right off he was in a heap of trouble.

"I'd gone from having a pretty good day relaxing to suddenly being on life support in about thirty seconds," Joe says with shaking his head. "It was crazy."

To the southeast of Block Island there's a rounded sea buoy that NOAA maintains. Aside from its steel construction, it'd be the ideal tennis ball for a beginner player with its three foot diameter and electric yellow color. It sits out there in about 162 feet of water riding the seas and diligently recording all matter of data. Despite its faithful service, it's assigned the very clinical station identification number 44097. In the lexicon of the industry, if you wanted to buy one of these specialized buoys, you'd ask for a "Waverider Buoy" and you'd better be prepared to pay more than $25,000. There are directional and non-directional buoys, but they share the same basic guts in that they contain an accelerometer, weather instruments and the ability to broadcast packets of information loaded with observational data.

At around the time Joe was considering his plight and the "Rock Bottom" was scurrying riderless back to the barn, 44097 recorded a water temperature of about 73 degrees Fahrenheit and a wave height of around three feet and a dominant wave period of around nine seconds. The wave period is the time between swells. It's how fast the waves go up and down, or, if you're out there swimming around, it's the time between the waves hitting you. 44097 is on the other side of Block Island from where Joe was swimming, but its recordings are pretty consistent with Joe's recollections.

"Right away, I was getting smacked pretty good with waves. It was like, paddle, paddle, kick, kick, wave, wave, wash, rinse and repeat," Joe explains. "That was a huge issue. I couldn't get a break from the water. I was constantly getting a bunch of water dumped on top of me 'cause I couldn't keep myself high enough in the water."

And that problem of being doused with seawater all night long was only going to get worse. The reams of data that spill forth from 44097 portray a sea intent on keeping Joe wet. By the early morning hours of July 18th, the dominant wave period had contracted more than half with a reading of 4.13 seconds and a wave height that exceeded three feet. In other words, by the time you've finished the last sentence and gotten through the next is about the time between waves. Aside from trying to keep his head above water, this kind of roiling sea made it exponentially more difficult for any kind of rescue to spot Joe. It's one thing trying to spot a coconut in a mill pond and quite another to spot a coconut in a roiling sea at night. Remarkably, all of these considerations were weighed by Joe.

"Yea, I thought about all that crap in the beginning," he says in response to my question. "Early on I sort of figured there was a chance that my boat would run up somewhere and someone would see my wallet and my keys and my phone and figure I'd gone over and they'd start a search. That was like the first thing I told myself that helped keep me calm. And I knew that the conditions weren't great, but I told myself if I can keep up and they get looking for me, there's a chance. That glimmer of hope kept me going, you know?"

And going and going.

Around 183 years earlier, Rhode Island's daily newspaper the Providence Journal was first published. The locals ask the diner waitress for a "ProJo" and it's proudly billed as "America's oldest daily newspaper in continuous publication." Like a mother hen, on the early evening of July 17, 2012, the ProJo reported that "a 23-foot lobster boat heading west toward Point Judith ran aground on Green Hill Beach with no one aboard." It went on to explain that the Coast Guard had dispatched a forty-seven foot lifeboat, a fast response vessel and a Jayhawk helicopter as well as having rerouted another vessel to assist in the search.

Sure enough, Joe's spooked horse had missed the barn, skittered across the evening surf and driven itself with high-pitched engine whine and scrape of fiberglass deep onto a stretch of ocean beach in South Kingstown, Rhode Island. It's a little patch of beach bordered with classic dunes and accessible down a winding sandy path at the end of the bucolic Green Hill Beach Road. Joe tells me that he'd heard that the husband and wife who'd found his boat had foregone a movie night to have a picnic, a scenario I don't doubt is true given the allure of that fat summer evening. A Coast Guard press release notes having received a telephone call from a woman which might seem to confirm this bit of gossip. Still, when Joe tells you, there's an undercurrent of anguish no doubt at the realization of the fortuity of the circumstances.

"I'm telling you," Joe says leaning back and stretching. "I know that spot where the "Rock Bottom" ran aground and if that couple hadn't been there, no one would've seen my boat where it was 'till the next morning and that wouldn't have worked. No way. I wouldn't be sitting here talking to you. It's crazy, man."

The Coast Guard reports having received a "relayed 911" call at approximately 7:30 p.m. on Tuesday evening. At this point, Joe estimates that he'd been in the drink for about two and half hours, or, 150 minutes. If you mess around and apply a dominant wave period of every nine seconds, that's something like 999 waves having passed over and around Joe before the Coast Guard machine first got going.

When I was working in the commercial marine sector in the late eighties and early nineties, the Coast Guard was running the stuffing out of old equipment. Good boats with good maintenance plans, but old boats and tired iron. On July 17, 2012, the Coast Guard had already taken delivery of something like 117 new forty-seven foot motor lifeboats. These are great looking craft designed to replace their work-weary fleet of forty-four foot vessels. With an all-aluminum hull and superstructure, 870 horsepower and a less than ten second self-righting capability, they are the Coast Guard's standard lifeboats.[7] The very look of these lifeboats conveys a sense of security. Broad across the stern with a short, smug bow, they have two massive exhaust ports on either side from which the two-tone snarl of

---

[7] For those wonky over such things, the following 47' MLB's details are offered: Twin Detroit Diesel Electronically Control (DDEC) 6V92TA Turbo Aftercooled, 2-Stroke, Right-Hand Rotation, 92 cu. in. per cylinder. 435 BHP each @ 2100 RPMs. The 47' MLB has a maximum speed of twenty-five knots, cruises at twenty knots and swings twin, four-bladed propellers each of which is a little over two feet in diameter. As equipped it has a length of forty-eight feet and eleven inches, a beam of fifteen feet and a draft of four feet, six inches. With seven watertight compartments, it's rated for thirty-foot seas, maximum winds of fifty knots and surf twenty-feet in height. Indeed, an awesome vessel.

their Detroit Diesel power issues. Like how the ear tunes itself to the funny tim-tam pattern of a Harley, a Detroit Diesel claims the honors of being one of the few diesel engine manufacturers to produce a two-stroke high speed engine.[8] The resulting sound is unlike any other diesel; a rapid percussion that rattles away like a Gatling gun. It's a sound of fire trucks and nighttime rescues, of big busses and the pulse of a city, and of hospital generators and the warm glow of emergency lighting. Any search engine will play you a clip of the Detroit Diesel's famous tune and it'll surely cause some memory to surface; it's the background sound of memorable moments in all of our lives.

The forty-seven foot motor lifeboat that got underway for Joe was stationed in Point Judith. It's an awkward arrangement with the lifeboat riding a dock across the ferry terminal just east of the old Dutch Inn and its crew mustering at the Point Judith lighthouse station. The Coast Guard crew rides a blue van down the winding mile or so between the station and the dock pressing fast on the curves, wheeling into the gravel lot with a splash of stone, stumbling out and sprinting down the dock. There's a ready crew that's already got the engines warmed up and the Detroit Diesels are clutched in and a swimming pool or so worth of water gets shoved aside as the lifeboat powers for the breakwater.

Joe was naked now; white flesh paddling away in a great puddle of green seawater. He'd shed his t-shirt early on believing that it was making it harder to swim and then thinking he'd be able to wave it at some passing craft and then letting it

---

[8] Internal combustion engines come in two flavors; two stroke and four stroke. A two-stroke engine completes a full power cycle in one revolution meaning that the piston sucks in fuel and air, fires, descends rotating the crankshaft, rises forcing out the exhaust, sucks in fuel and air, fires, etc. Interestingly, two-stroke engines can work in any engine orientation making their use appropriate in a vessel (like MLB 47274) that is designed to endure a capsizing event.

slip away realizing the weighted cotton only threatened the outcome. He'd tried to use his shorts in the way they teach you in the big Y.M.C.A. pools. For a makeshift lifejacket, the instructors sagely say, knot the legs, swirl it over your head filling the inseam with air and cinch the waist. Two tries and a quarter liter of ingested seawater later, Joe let the shorts float away and focused on a pattern of paddling and kicking. Just enough to keep him afloat while reserving the stamina to kick his way through the bigger waves. There was an incessant rush and press of ocean.

"It was like it was a game of wits, you know," Joe says sucking on his Bud bottle. "I don't know, anytime I started to get in a zone, I'd get smacked by a wave. It was tough finding that middle ground and it kept feeling like I was falling down on the canvas. It was like I kept getting hit. I don't know, maybe that was the rhythm, right? Knocked to my knees, shake it off, stand up and take some more punishment."

Like the Waverider buoy, it's the same with the Coast Guard's motor lifeboats. Only a sterile numerical designation graces their transom; well not that sterile. The first two numerals represent the vessel's length. And so, as that beautiful Tuesday receded into tomorrow, motor lifeboat 47274 with its crew of five plowed a phosphorous mustache of seawater as it headed into a dark night to look for a man overboard. That is, to look for a person presenting a profile the size of a floating coconut.

Aboard 47274, there was the serious eyed machinist technician, Keith, the coxswain Andrew with his laid back demeanor, Justin the self-assured engineer, a grinning Chris who was new to the Point Judith station and Bosun's Mate Anthony all manning a machine that costs around $1.24 Million to buy and untold tens of thousands more to crew, equip and operate. They're young with optimistic faces yet unscarred by the successes and failures of time. Fortuity, training and the United States Government cobbled together this crew from places as far away as Texas, Ohio, and Idaho. The individual motivations among them for joining the Coast Guard vary although some simply wanted to work on the sea. I put the issue of motivation to each of them directly and halfway around the table one of them sat up in his chair and told me something to the effect that he'd joined the Coast Guard because it was the only military branch he believed that was about saving people as opposed to killing them. He probably said it more eloquently than I'm recounting, but there seemed to me to be collective agreement among the others on that statement. There seemed to me to be a genuine passion among them for doing something that helped people. Yes, of course, other military branches shoulder tremendous burdens in the furtherance of protecting this Country and its people and, yes, other military branches engage in many humanitarian efforts, but those activities are not, to my understanding, part of their DNA. The Coast Guard is different. It wears a lot of hats, but wound tight in its genetic fiber is the idea of saving souls at sea. Go ahead and look at the federal statute entitled "Preserving Coast Guard Mission Performance" (6 U.S.C. § 648). It lists "Marine Safety" and "Search and Rescue" as the Coast Guard's top two missions. To give you a sense of the depth of its commitment to search and rescue, in 2010 the Coast Guard ground out 64,273 hours on in its soul-saving work.In 2012, they recorded 3,804 lives saved and 20,510 search and rescue missions. And heck, the Guard's been doing this for 222 years![9]

In the parlance of the brass, that's a "mission statement" that stands uniquely by itself and I regret that I didn't give that element of the Coast Guard more consideration in my youth as it

---

[9] The Coast Guard's marching song "*Semper Paratus*" contains this line in the third verse: "To sink the foe or save the maimed." I think that line neatly illustrates the Coast Guard's unique standing.

may, too, have affected my career choice.[10] On a bitter cold winter evening seated around a table at the Point Judith Coast Guard Station, its windows facing the inky blackness of a far-stretching Atlantic Ocean, that specific motivation caught me off guard. It was a refreshing reveal of the sort of basics that I like to think built this grand Country. Those words spoken so earnestly and quickly were a solvent that scrubbed some of the dulling lacquer of the Guantanamo Bay and Abu Ghraib kind from my view. Those words summed up America's might, not the firepower of the high-flying drone or the thuggery of war. That single comment in response to a passing question restored immensely in me the idea that America's might is its willingness to help others and to give hope where none might otherwise exist. Still, lounging in chairs with the odors of an awaiting dinner of pork chops and mashed potatoes urging the meeting's end, I don't think the crew of motor lifeboat 47274 thought much about deeper meanings. Like Joe says, they were just telling me like it was.[11]

Joe had a plan. It was sort of a two-pronged plan. First, he was going to keep afloat and second, he was going to swim to Block Island. He'd swim, he'd figure, right into New Harbor and pad up the sandy beach in his birthday suit and announce to the world that he'd lived. No big deal. He was good in the water, he told himself. It's just a swim. Get going. Kick it in gear.

And it'd be so damn doable if the sea would just work with me.

---

[10] Whilst there's no saving lives in the author's chosen profession as an admiralty attorney, there is the belief that his advocacy does help further people's interests; that his advocacy does make a difference for small businesses and people with maritime claims.

[11] As a point of accuracy, the crewmember identified as "Anthony" was not in attendance and the author has not met with or spoken to this crewmember.

"What I wanted to do was keep myself heading in a direction toward BI [Block Island]," Joe says. "And so I just swam as best I could. Sometimes it was me on my side; sometimes it was me just kicking and stroking away. Steady is what I was aiming for. Nice breathing. Everything was about the breathing; I really focused on my breathing. No matter what, I told myself to keep moving, but it was tough. You're so freaking low in the water that it's hard to orient. But I had this plan to keep myself up as long as I could so someone could maybe spot me and to swim toward New Harbor. I pretty much blanked everything else out and kept focused on those two things. That, and the breathing."

"What about sharks," I ask like a lurid tabloid reporter. "Being out in those waters, was that something that scared you?"

He brushes the question off with a half shake of his head and a curt reply.

"Never thought about it. I was thinking about things I could control. My breathing, swimming and trying to get to Block Island was pretty much it."

Months later while meeting with the 47274's crew, I got an equally curt response from Andrew when I asked him about each person's rank. It seems that once the five of them are aboard the lifeboat, they're all crew. Aside from the coxswain and engineer, it seems like they basically shed their rank on the dock and work together as crew to complete the mission. They weren't sure what they had on their hands, but they were eager to lend a hand. When Andrew throttled up the 47274's throttles, the pulse and howl of the big twin four-hundred plus horsepower diesels echoed around the Harbor of Refuge's rock jetties.

Pulling the wheel around the big lifeboat leaned over and galloped away from the direction where Joe was blinking his eyes clear of seawater and toward Green Hill Beach laying a big foamy trail.

And so it was like two strangers on a dance floor. All they needed was the right tempo, pace and patience and maybe good fortune would have them meet up.

Chapter Eight

"Waning Crescent" would be a corker of a name for a sailboat. There's something elegant in the phrase when it's applied to the long and shapely curve of a hull with a towering rig of blinding white sail. The phrase is decidedly less elegant when applied to the lunar phase of the date on which you've elected to paddle around the Atlantic Ocean hoping to be spotted. Such was Joe's predicament.

The evening of July 17, 2012 was characterized by what astronomers call an "old moon." That's a moon that's getting smaller and smaller moons reflect less ambient light making the sea dark and oily. When you research these things, you learn that only three percent of the moon is illuminated in that phase. If only Joe had rescheduled his swim for early August, he would've had a full moon with one hundred percent illumination. The ocean waters would have been bathed in a creamy glow instead of coal pitch darkness.

The crew of motor lifeboat 47274 remembered it was dark night, but it wasn't to gripe. It was just another element to address and overcome. Once a little ways clear of the West Gap of Point Judith's Harbor of Refuge, they slowed up and began a shoreline search as they headed west along the coastline toward Green Hill Beach.

"You never know," one of the 47274's crew explains. "It could be that the guy jumped off at the last minute 'cause of a stuck rudder or throttle, so that was our first attempt. We wanted to move along the coast and see if we could find somebody up close."

It was a belt and suspenders kind of logic. Start with the obvious and easiest and then work toward the more remote and more difficult. They took turns standing watch on the open bridge, fourteen feet or so above the seawater's surface. They swung spotlights and worked a set of night vision goggles awaiting more information and direction from the Coast Guard's shore side operations center. Every one of them had worked together in the past except for Chris, but he has an easy way that suggests someone who fits in easily. They powered along, rocking back and forth, straining eyes and running on adrenaline. This was why they'd signed up, right?

Ashore on the street named "Summer," Brenda Lee Gross, Joe's wife was alone in their house. They weren't living together on July 17, 2012 and I'd speculate that she was probably suffering the separation trying to find some balance in her life after the change of circumstances. At around the time the 47274 was steadily nosing its way down the coast toward Green Hill Beach, Brenda was curled up on her couch talking to her sister.

"I was on my cell and I usually don't answer other calls, but our son Jacob was working at a camp in New Hampshire and I hadn't heard from him in a while and I thought it might be him calling," she nervously explains. You get the sense that the sharp events of that day haven't been softened by the months since.

She answered the phone with the expectancy of a mother wanting to hear her son's voice. Instead she heard the tin tongue of the local police dispatcher. It was a message conveyed without assurance or positive note. She remembers the dispatcher telling her that Joe's boat came up on Green Hill Beach at full throttle and without anyone aboard. His cell phone and wallet, the dispatcher added, were recovered inside. She brings her hands together as she recalls this moment; hands sun-marked by so many summer months she'd spent aboard the boat with her husband. Her hands seem to tremble with the recollection.

"I knew that was a really bad sign," she says her hair falling forward and those nervous hands working to push it back.

The dispatcher said he'd call back, the line disconnected and Brenda was alone in her house. It seems like an awful way to convey information. Separated, divorced or still madly in love, it seems like an awful way to learn of such news. It seems like a cruel joke, like a head-on car accident in the midst of a routine errand. Lesser people would have succumbed hopelessly, but whether it was her time with Joe, or, her own constitution, Brenda rallied. She wanted to tell Joe's family about what had happened, but not the way she'd learned. She didn't want a mere telephone connection letting them know that their son, their brother was lost at sea.

Summertime being what it is, everyone was everywhere. Joe's parents, Joe and Kay, were at a picnic and his two sisters, Marsha and Nadine, were in different locales around town. It took some time before everyone got together, but they're a tight family and there was an urgency to the situation and soon everyone was at Joe's place on Summer Street. She told them what she knew, but she can't recall the scene well. I imagine her with palms pressed together and skin tight across her face blurting out bits and pieces and trying hard to keep it together.

The mid-summer evening temperatures were in the low nineties and the shore-side humidity and heat was oppressive. New Englanders, I think, take their cold better than their heat and Brenda explained that all her windows were open and everyone was sort of moving slowly, like they were in a sticky treacle of physical and mental discomfort. Brenda reached for the telephone and called the dispatcher back and learned from the same tin voice that the matter had been turned over to the Coast Guard. She hung up not knowing the significance.

"It was like 100 degrees in the house," Brenda says. "And we'd had this skunk under the porch all summer and now the only thing anyone could smell was skunk and one of Joe's sister's was crying and it was just, just horrible."

And then the Woods Hole Coast Guard Station telephoned. She answered on the first ring.

"He was just the nicest, calmest, most professional guy," she says huffing a big breath. "I think his name was Commander Smith and I just can't say enough about him. It was such a contrast from the dispatcher that I'd talked to. This guy told me what they knew, what they were doing and set up a time to call me back and let me know the progress they were making. It was like he gave me some hope, you know?"

Hope, it's what makes the world go around.

I must be representative of an older and dumber generation because I was surprised that nary a single crewmember aboard the motor lifeboat 47274 smoked, dipped or otherwise relied on tobacco to keep them sharp. They were universal in telling me it was adrenaline alone. They even eschewed energy drinks in favor of granola bars and water. It was interesting; interesting to learn that where some might have considered the endeavor fruitless, the crew of the 47274 was passionate. When you listen to them, this wasn't a going-through-the-paces group. They talk about watching each other for signs of fatigue. They talk about eyes strained by squinting at curling waves and foaming water. They talk about hearts racing only to learn that the maddening glint of white flesh was the shiny curve of a lobster pot. Like the motivation speakers preach, the crew of the 47274 visualized success from the inception of their voyage and they pursued it mercilessly into the night.

They have the lingo down, too. It's like any profession where the industry lexicon filters into your thinking. Once the search down to Green Hill Beach came up "negative," they were "tasked" with a "parallel search."

There's whole classes and bound volumes on the theory of search and rescue. This isn't you chasing around the neighborhood after your dog. Search and rescue at this level is a distillate of scientific theory where probability outcomes are expressed in nausea-inducing equations and the likelihood of success is dependent on a series of variables. With graphs of probability density distributions and chapter titles identifying such mysteries as detection models, lateral range curves and sweep width, it's clear that the Coast Guard is very wonky about its search and rescue.[12]

A parallel search pattern is, as the title gives away, a series of parallel searches. The easiest way to conceptualize this kind of search is to imagine a large lawn and you behind a mower. The yard is the search area and each time you get to the end of the yard and spin the mower around, you've completed one leg of the search. Aboard motor lifeboat 47274, the end of each search leg was achieved when they reached a prescribed waypoint. That is, a waypoint is a specific location delineated by a latitudinal and longitudinal coordinate and so when you reach this coordinate, you pull the wheel around, motor a short distance on the cross leg, pull the wheel around again and head back down the "lawn" to your next waypoint. Each search leg has a certain amount of defined distance or spread between the last search leg which is referred to as "track space." For those of you who don't have a lawn, don't mow a lawn, or, didn't follow

---

[12] By way of historical note, despite the human race having spent ions searching for things whether it be the lowly flint, coin or enemy, it wasn't until the early 1940's that empirical models for visually detecting things (like warships) were developed. Whilst the author claims no talent for mathematics, having parsed various writings on the subject, the reader may be relatively assured that this stuff is complicated.

my horticultural explanation, the below diagram depicts a parallel search pattern:

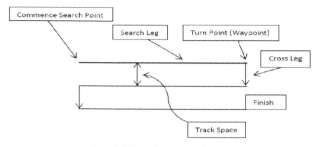

-- Parallel Search Pattern Example --

The Coast Guard considers the parallel search to be the most common search method and I'd venture the most successful for covering a large piece of real estate quickly.Plus, with a universal reliance on Global Positioning Systems ("GPS"), it's an easy search to assign and (in theory) execute. However, as with many things that look slick on the pixelated screen, the parallel search's translation to actual searching is another matter. This is tough stuff; tough, tiring stuff particularly so on the evening of July 17 and morning hours of July 18.

First off, the seas were rough. Just as Joe had tried to impress on me months before, when I sat down with motor lifeboat 47274's crew they were universal in explaining that it was a snotty evening. The seas were rough enough that the Coast Guard's twenty-five foot vessel was getting knocked around. Without reference to the records, the crew I met with recollected a four to six foot chop to the man. (Upon refreshing their recollection from the records it was noted that the seas were recorded as two to six feet.)

Second, the curling and foaming sea wreaked havoc with the night vision optics. From what I gathered, all anyone wearing them saw was a lot of shiny white with the likelihood of picking out Joe's head being pretty slim; no way it was going to happen was how I recall one of the crew describing the night vision.

Third, and undoubtedly odd to the unfamiliar, the ocean evening was cool. More than one member of the 47274's crew remarked on how chilly the evening became. From the author's experience running offshore at night, this is not an unusual circumstance despite the existence of otherwise oppressive temperatures inland.

Fourth, search patterns are boring. Not boring in the realm of a mid-winter Sunday afternoon, but a boring akin to the tedium that accompanies any repetitive task be it assembling sneakers or studying ledger entries. Yes, the adrenaline of finding a human in distress may keep your eyes wide, but the monotony of studying square miles of empty ocean is mind numbing.

Finally, the time had run long. To their credit, not one of the crew of the 47274 would concede that as the night drew old and a new morning dawned, they must have felt a sense of futility. There had to have been a sense of wanting to just finish up and get home, I urged. But, again to the man, they looked at me with a sense of incredulousness. This was an important endeavor, a human's life was at stake and while the probability graphs might not have looked strong, they were looking as hard at the eleventh hour as the first.

Whether I'm jaded with age, or, softened by too much Scotch and good eats, I find this a remarkable feat. Keeping up hope friend, is as hard if not harder than conjuring hope.

For Joe, his hope was buoyed by the Coast Guard's search. It's a remarkable thing, but I suspect that part of the Coast Guard's motivation in throwing assets at a search and rescue is to provide a visual cue for the lost. In speaking with

Joe, it's clear that his spirits were immensely improved by seeing vessel activity, by seeing (and smelling the kerosene flavored exhaust) of a low flying Coast Guard helicopter and by knowing that someone was on the dance floor. Still, it got frustrating.

"It was nuts," Joe says shaking his head. "They'd bring this helicopter over me and I could smell its freaking kerosene burners and they'd swing by and move past. I just didn't have anything to try and get their attention. If only I'd had a light or something to catch their attention."

I asked the 47274's crew about this in my maritime attorney sort of cross-examination way: "Didn't the Coast Guard helicopter have a FLIR [thermal imaging] system on it? Why'd they miss Joe? Were they sleeping at the switch?"

There's no need to narrate the response I received and suffice it to say that a human body's head and neck amount to about nine percent of their body mass hence there's very little temperature gradient for the FLIR to identify. Moreover, Joe was being continually doused by seawater which would have lowered his temperature signature.

"I just kept swimming," Joe says. "I just kept paddling away and that was about what it had come down to 'cause I couldn't really do anything like floating because of the waves. I just kept swimming I was really thinking, and it's crazy when I look back, but I kept thinking I was getting closer to Old Harbor. It was like my reality was totally distorted."

So the Coast Guard have these portable buoys called Self Locating Random Marker Buoys and you can imagine us sitting around that table on that cold night at the Point Judith Coast Guard Station and the 47274's crew bickering over this acronym. Anyway, the point is that months later they'd been called in to review the data from just such a buoy that had been deployed in Joe's search and the damn thing had gone around

Block Island confounding any of the tidal predictions. In other words, Joe was in a big whirl pool being sucked and tugged along by the sweep of the tidal currents. His conceptualization of where'd he been swimming was as topsy-turvy as the seas in which he was battling.

But still, while the dance floor was wide and long, they were getting closer.

Chapter Nine

To a New Englander, seagulls are as prevalent and underfoot as pigeons in a city. Gulls crowd docks, strut through parking lots, stand watch atop lampposts, bob past harbor entrances and shout and scream their descending akk-crawww notes at each other. For the boat owner, however, the touristy post-card image of the seagull is nothing but slick promotion. Gulls ravage clean boat decks with droppings, bits of half-eaten crab detritus and chunks of clam shells. They're smart birds and once they pry a thick-shelled mollusk free from a tidal flat, they swoop aloft, spot a drop zone and release the shell to shatter on the hard surface be it asphalt or the AwlGrip paint job you're still paying for. I've grown up and around gulls and I've never taken a shine to them. I'd miss them if they weren't there as one would miss an old oak felled in a storm, but not the way you'd miss a dog or a summer robin. There's something hard and savage about a seagull's fierce beak and carrion colored eyes. And what Joe told me about the seagulls he saw as he paddled along didn't do anything to foster my love of these feathered creatures.

Curiously, they're all types of gulls and the term is sort of synonymous with "ducks" in that they're all kinds of ducks or all sorts of nuts or differing models of cars. In North America, you have the Black-Legged Kittiwake with its dark smudged head, the Herring Gull dressed in its slate colored plumage and the Laughing Gull named for its distinctive call. And these are just but a small sampler of the many varieties and types including the LarusMarinus, or, the Great-Black-backed Gull which is not only the largest of its genus, but the largest darn gull in the world. Weighing upwards of five pounds and with a wingspan around five feet, they range as far south as the Caribbean and even onto the northern coasts of South America. These are genetically superior beasts living as long as twenty-seven years in the wild and as long as forty-four years in captivity. But ask around and you'll hear the common sentiment that they're also the meanest of the lot.

Sometime in the early morning of July 18, the Black-backed gulls spotted Joe.

"It was in the very predawn light," Joe says. "And I remember these gulls fluttering overhead. They'd come right down to a foot or so above me and beat their wings. I'd been swimming for so long at that point, that all I could really do was curse at them. If they'd come right down on me; if they'd had a try at my eyes like they do with dead fish, I don't think I could have done anything. I would've drowned, I was that close."

We're sitting across from each other at a varnished table in the Westerly Yacht Club, Joe and I, when he tells me about the gulls. It's a late fall evening and the bar behind us is full of locals. A warm murmur of camaraderie fills the space. Joe sits with his back to it all. He looks down at the table and pulls his beer closer. His shoulders are rounded and he doesn't look healthy. He looks tired. He runs a hand across the top of his head and takes a funny, slanting breath. He shifts and then asks me if I want another cup of coffee. The wound is still fresh. You get the sense that no matter what gauze he uses to wrap those memories with whether its alcohol or women or the hustle of life, the wounds are slow healing. No one gets that close to the edge of the abyss without coming back bloodied and bruised.

As near as I can calculate, around the time Joe was wrestling with the gulls, Brenda was curled up in the bottom of a shower. Everyone had gone home, she'd insisted. There was nothing to do but await the Coast Guard's hourly update call. The same call with the solid confidence of the Coast Guard officer, but always with the same news that there was no news. The water fell in torrents from the showerhead, pelting off her back and drowning out the world in white noise. She had a deep faith in Joe's abilities, but as the minutes bled into hours and the hours into the start of a new day, whatever hope she'd fought to keep waned and faded. I imagine she watched the water puddle and pool around her feet and disappear down the drain and it reminded her of the loss she'd have to accept. It was such a damn crappy way to go and such a damn crappy time to go. I suspect she shook with pain at the things said and unsaid and reality of losing Joe in the midst of their own, very personal struggle with the direction of their relationship. And then there was the son. She hadn't told her son that his father was missing because he was safely away at camp and, really, what good could come of it? But now, with morning nearly on the doorstep, she'd have to talk to Jacob.

Aboard motor lifeboat 47274, the Detroit Diesels kept crackling along. The sound of the exhaust changed timbre as the vessel heeled and rocked in the seas. Sometimes one exhaust was lower than the other, sometimes an exhaust echoed off a curling swell and sometimes when the transom was level they hit a pitch-perfect note. They were mowing miles and miles of ocean. They'd been assigned five parallel search patterns each pattern the result of a sophisticated affair involving, among other things, consideration of on-scene conditions, tidal currents and the Coast Guard's vast experience. The specific parallel search pattern to undertake would be transmitted to the 47274 from the Coast Guard's New England Sector located in Woods Hole, Massachusetts. As the time dragged on, the parallel searches changed to accommodate how the Coast Guard predicted a swimmer would be tugged and pulled by the ocean.

They'd completed four parallel searches and the specter of fatigue had to have been creeping across the 47274's crew. I questioned the crew as to how they remained alert and they told me with an easy explanation that made me think of a high school game on the hard woods. It turns out it was a self-policing affair where the team members work together to ensure everyone's pulling their weight. On the half-hour or so, they'd rotate watch standing positions changing tasks while one or two of them would steal below into the 47274's cabin and huddle away from the raw ocean breeze. The search light was still sweeping across the ocean top, the night-vision goggles were still being swung back and forth their glow revealing a wide and empty expanse.

"We were on the second to last leg of our last search pattern," they explain. "We were getting ready to be relieved by another crew." Anthony was at the helm, Andrew was the starboard lookout and the 47274 was plowing along its running lights reflecting red and green against the breaking white ocean chop. I watch their faces when they tell me what happened next and you can see that where for Joe the memory hurts, for this young crowd the memory remains full of voltage.

"For whatever reason, it's like four in the morning and the fishing fleet from Point Judith is heading out. They're all steaming out 'cause I guess that's the time they usually do, I don't know," recounts one of the 47274's crew. "We're all on the lookout deck and it's chilly and this one fishing boat is in our way and not moving and we'd tried everything to get their attention and hailing them on Channel 16 and nothing. And so we made the choice to alter course to port because if we didn't we'd have hit them."

All of the 47274's crew is contributing to the narrative and there's a level of disbelief in their eyes as they explain what happened next.

"So we come to port and we'd been seeing nothing but whitecaps all night and then all of sudden there's something different," Andrew says. "The green tint from the starboard running light hit him and I knew right then I saw him. It was like after looking so long, the green glow of light caused him to stick out and all of a sudden Anthony and I heard him shouting. We both heard him."

And then, as those special moments are apt to bring out, there's gentle disagreement between the 47274's crew over the timing, over who saw what when, and over who did what next. But it's an understandable squabble of a familial quality and mostly powered by the clambering enthusiasm of wanting to be accurate while wanting to have been the one in the immediate fray. But it's all unnecessary because listening to them recount the moment a half year later it's clear that they'd all found him. That they'd all worked together to find a floating coconut in some of the worst conditions you could've ever presented. They could have jogged to port and turned to each other to gripe and squeeze a short laugh over the fishing boat's refusal to move, but they turned to port and kept vigilant. It is a remarkable example of executing one's duty.

For Joe, time was short. That's easy to write and it's an expression that's been used too much in the past, but how else to explain his physiological and mental state? It was just about the eleventh hour and in the dream-world that increasingly pervades a survival situation, Joe was utterly lost. He'd seen the lights of the fishing fleet and had wrongly believed he'd completed his swim.

"I thought I was near New Harbor," he says laughing. "I thought I'd done it that I'd almost finished swimming and I kept thinking about my feet scraping the bottom and collapsing on the beach. And then I hear this really loud noise and it's like this awesome whaaawwwww noise," he says raising his voice. "I thought it was a plane. Really. I thought it was one of those C-130's doing a low pass over me. Man, I was so out of it and then a boat's next to me and they've got these boat hooks in their hands and I was like 'No way, I got nothing.'"[13]

---

[13] Interestingly, Joe tells me that when he saw the Coast Guard holding boathooks instead of, say, a life ring he was convinced that they thought he was dead. This understanding was disputed by the 47274's crew which explains that the boathooks were simply close at

But memories are fickle and we all spackle history with our own plaster of facts and make ourselves sound better than we did at the time. And maybe when the gaping maw of death is as near as it was for Joe, even months later pressing back against the reality of the moment is to be expected.

Joe didn't say much, the 47274's crew tells me. Sure, they grabbed a couple of boathooks because they were close at hand, but what Joe said to them was a plea not an instruction.

"I'm very weak, please help me. I'm so weak," they remember him saying.

Everyone aboard the 47274 was on deck and a couple of them were in position in a recess cutout in the side of the lifeboat that allows you to stand almost at the water's surface. They grabbed Joe and pulled him aboard. It took three of them to get him clear of the sea. Joe wasn't dead, but he was deadweight.

Once aboard, the crew hurried Joe into the 47274's survivor's compartment and tried warming him up while pushing the throttles forward and winding out the Detroit Diesels. Like any good team, I had the impression that the 47274's crew wasn't calling the game over until they'd delivered a breathing Joe to the dock and an awaiting ambulance. Despite the jubilation, these were measured professionals who worried shock and hypothermia.

"He was cold and weak and he was shivering so much he couldn't stand," the crew tells me. "He kept asking how long he'd been in the water, but we didn't want to tell him because we didn't want him to go further into shock."

---

hand and that deploying a life ring or the like would not have been practical given the circumstances.

Joe was delivered ashore. He was tucked into an ambulance and ferried to the South County Hospital. I asked the 47274's crew what they did next. How'd they celebrate?

"When we found him and he was alive; it was like a pretty good sigh of relief," they tell me. "But at that point in time, by the time we got back it was like 4:30 in the morning and we'd been up since six a.m. the day before so the adrenaline rush came down and we went to bed."[14]

"Job description fulfilled, right?" I say and they all laugh in agreement.

Joe doesn't say much on the way out of the Point Judith Coast Guard station. He'd brought his son with him. He's a rangy, quiet kid in boat shoes who looks like he's in the throes of those years where you don't know who you are or where you're going. I wonder what he thinks about his father's ordeal. I don't ask.

We're expecting a winter storm and we leave the station's warmly dinner smells and walk across the parking lot with a chill wind shaking the main gate and rattling the flagpole's lines. Behind us, there's a sweeping view of the waters where Joe struggled for eleven hours, but Joe doesn't turn to look. He makes a beeline for his car, chunks the door shut and I watch him drive away between the sand dunes and away from the ocean.

---

[14] The Command Duty Officer of Sector Southeastern New England at the time, Scott Backholm, issued a statement following the rescue of Joe Gross stating: "Many Coast Guard assets came together with a team effort to save this man." While this story focuses its attention in part on the 47274's crew, the reader should understand that the crew of the 47274 repeatedly made such similar statements when speaking with this author and universally gave credit to the Coast Guard as a whole.

I let my car idle and sit staring into the inky blackness of the Atlantic Ocean. I wonder how something like this scars you mentally. I wonder if each of us are allotted a reservoir of hope that drains lower through life and, if so, how much is left in Joe's tank. I wonder if a high-school English teacher would find the green running light that flashed across Joe's face reminiscent of that old saw of a story The Great Gatsby where the object of hope is a green light.[15] I wonder if it's ironic that the official motto of the State of Rhode Island where Joe lives is simply and plainly "Hope." Me, you or somebody far more competent in such things could probably unravel and explore the deeper meanings of Joe's struggle, but I tend to believe that for Joe in the end, he'll be alright and it'll just go down as a swim.

---

[15] F. Scott Fitzgerald (2004).The Great Gatsby.New York: Scribner Reissue Edition.

Chapter Ten

To sail the Atlantic, to round the Cape of Good Hope, to clamber aboard a life raft, to step into the sea from a foundering vessel are crystalline moments. They are the sharp ridges that as you gaze off your life's transom you'll always see. But those ridges don't have to be salty to remain vivid. Joe's story isn't unique because many of you have survived or will survive your own personal eleven hours of treading water. Life is rarely a smooth evening sail and the lessons of Joe's experience can serve as your own, personal life vest.

An important first lesson and what struck me the most in writing this story is Joe's clinical and selfless approach to surviving. That is, Joe didn't allow himself to wallow in the horror of the moment and he consciously recognized the importance of not dwelling on what his death would mean. He did not suffer thoughts about his impending loss of life. He did not call out to a creator for salvation, or, bemoan the choices that landed him in the drink. He didn't simper over the loss of a future be it lost game nights, lovers not bedded, parties missed, family milestones or what have you. Instead, with a mechanical-like logic, Joe tamped-down his emotions and clinically analyzed his options. It was as if Joe's steadfast persistence through a life lead under his own terms had left him with a script detailing how to handle such a situation. Drawing on his background and experiences, Joe was able to follow that script and keep himself alive until he was rescued. In that sense, Joe teaches us a powerful lesson.

We live in a world of selfish indulgence. The singular importance of the individual overwhelms our lives. We are constantly bombarded by the preening and primping of YouTube stars and media darlings. Comfort, style and attention seem to rule the day. We're dulled by our own seeming self-importance and flagrantly promote our singular existence as a motivating life force. For so many, there seems to be an arrogant confidence that our mere existence is the penultimate life accomplishment. The problem with this way of thinking is that despite all this focus on yourself, you're really playing to an audience and survival isn't about an audience. Survival is about having the grit, determination and confidence to fight when the odds are against you and those qualities are only really plumbed by knowing yourself. That "script" that I mention Joe relied upon in surviving this ordeal didn't write itself, it took years of personal accomplishments (no matter how small) to develop a storyline Joe could rely upon in his hour of need.

When Joe splashed free of his vessel, it was his own self confidence built atop a lifetime of accomplishing things that kept him buoyant. Sure, Joe's accomplishments were of a small order, but they were his. They were a commitment to a job, a genuine love and understanding of the outdoors and a steadfast persistence. Joe persists not through the encouragement of an audience, but through a belief in what he is able to accomplish.

The second lesson that seems clear is that the basic elements of survival depend on you. No matter how numerous your Twitter followers or voluminous your Facebook friends, your ability to overcome life's obstacles and survive is very much reliant upon your individual skills. Anyone who has suffered a serious physical injury and endured countless hours of rehabilitation is familiar with this teaching. The therapist can show you the exercise, but it's up to you to retrain your muscle. It's you who must learn to flex your arm or extend that knee. Likewise, those that have come through the suffering that accompanies the loss of another must ultimately realize that they alone own their loss. The reassuring words of a grief counselor and the warmth of a religious conviction can swaddle your soul, but it is you alone that must fashion a way to corral the loss and carry onward. In that sense, what Joe experienced was an intense exposure to the uncomfortable reality that we are very much alone. Joe did not have anything or anyone to rely upon.

He had no assurance that any rescue would be mounted because no one was expecting him. The only hope he had was in himself. He, alone, possessed the keys to his survival. It was up to Joe to decide whether he would live or die.

In that regard, it's striking that Joe's plan did not rank being rescued on the first tier. Instead, the primary goal of Joe's plan (no matter how insanely hopeful it may sound in hindsight) was to swim to New Harbor, Block Island. If in executing this plan he placed himself in a position where he might be rescued, so much the better. But the foundation of Joe's hope was this fundamental concept of responsibility to himself. He wasn't willing to huddle and await the possibility of the Calvary's arrival instead he took responsibility for his own survival.

"I knew pretty quick that I had a choice," he says flatly. "I could choose to live or I could die. It was sort of weirdly apparent that I'd probably die, but I chose life and told myself that I was going to get a plan together, follow the plan and I'd live. When I think about it, the whole plan thing was really clear to me too. I had this feeling that if I had a plan and stuck to it, I'd live."

There's another lesson that flows from what Joe says about coming up with your own plan and its related to this idea of taking responsibility for your own survival.

We're always preached to about how success is the result of teamwork. From grade school to business school, the concept of cultivating and relying on friendships is broadcast as the recipe for survival. Popularity is equated to success. Our society questions the loner, the mad scientist, the lone ranger, the spinster. But, there are all too many moments when we're balanced very much alone on a thin reed bridge high above dark waters. There are circumstances where the choice and initiative are yours alone. No matter the number of your friends nor intricacy of relationships, there are those choices where you, alone, must dig deep and reach for the grit that resides in each of us. And 'lo, like the preternatural grit that carries an infant through an unforgiving fever, or, like Elizabeth Barrow lifting her child free of the icy waters, you're filled with the power to do far more than what we expect or accept as possible. These are conquests and successes that do not depend on your network or social skills, but depend solely on what's inside your soul. When you huff your last breath whether in the screaming sound of twisted metal or the crackle of starched sheets, you're alone. We start and end our voyage very much alone and no matter of gloss can undo that stark reality. I believe that it's those of us who realize that empirical fact who will summit, who will survive, who will conquer and who don't drown.

Finally, there's nothing incredibly special about Joe. No superhuman capability. No greater lung capacity or mental acuity. He's an average guy and very much the common man save for his singular understanding that it takes independent grit to get places. Whether by nature or nurture, Joe knows that you rise and fall on your individual efforts. For Joe, that grit maybe lives closer to the bone than for many others. I don't possess the training or tools to fully unfold why Joe was able to dig so deep. I don't want to believe the cliché that he is a dying breed, but this potential beckons warmly. He does things and he refuses to live in a social unreality. He's taken punches and thrown some too. He's witnessed death first-hand. He's lived, loved, bled, fathered, and traveled. He's held jobs and lost them. He's seen death, missed opportunities, taken wrong turns, made friends, gained respect, helped others and lived life. I tend to believe that all of those colorful experiences add up to something and contribute to your perspective. I tend to believe that without cultivating life experiences, it becomes a lot harder to dig deep and find the grit necessary to survive. Without a richly populated mind full of all the whips and whirls that life brings, I believe you can't fully realize your potential.

And so, that's it. It was just a swim, but in that swim there lies an awful lot.

Prologue

At the time of this writing, a year hasn't yet passed since the ordeal. In my interactions with him, Joe appears to be in a good humor and remains devoted to the outdoors and the ocean. I can't predict (and am too respectful) to ask whether he and Brenda will get back together. If you're asking me to speculate, I'd say I'm not sure, but like surviving a fall overboard, I don't believe the passage of time improves the odds. I understand that in mid-February, 2013, the crew of 47274 received Coast Guard awards for their efforts in rescuing Joe. I'd glad to have seen that they were recognized and remain impressed by their professionalism. A couple of weeks ago, I was walking the docks in Point Judith, Rhode Island and heard with my own ears, the lovely sounds of Motor Lifeboat 47274, may it continue to do its good work for many years to come.

Oh, one more thing, Joe assures me that he doesn't venture aboard any floating craft without a lifejacket, ever.

Underway and making way.

--- John K. Fulweiler, Jr.

About the Author

John K. Fulweiler, Jr. is an experienced maritime attorney and is recognized as a Proctor-In-Admiralty by the Maritime Law Association of the United States. He has the helm of his own maritime law firm with its principal office in Newport, Rhode Island and which represents individuals and claimants on the East and Gulf Coasts. John possesses significant experience in prosecuting claims for maritime personal injury and wrongful death. In addition, John has pursued class action status in maritime product liability matters. Licensed to practice law in numerous jurisdictions including Rhode Island, New York and Florida, John also possesses practical maritime experience and is a licensed United States Coast Guard mariner. John is often in the media writing regularly for various maritime publications and appearing as an expert in maritime legal matters on television and radio broadcasts. John may be reached at **john@fulweilerlaw.com**, **www.saltwaterlaw.com**, or, via his Firm's toll-free number: **1-800-383-MAYDAY**.